From: Valerie
&
Aunt Angela
2015

Nursery Rhymes

ILLUSTRATED BY HILDA OFFEN

KINGFISHER

KINGFISHER
Larousse Kingfisher Chambers Inc.
95 Madison Avenue
New York, New York 10016

2 4 6 8 10 9 7 5 3 1

1BDR/1100/MIL/—/115MA

Some of the material in this book was previously published in
A Treasury of Mother Goose 1984 and *My Favorite Nursery Rhymes* 1987

ISBN 1-56619-246-3

Edited by Vanessa Clarke and Janice Lacock
Designed by Cathy Tincknell

Printed in Italy

CONTENTS

Sleep, Baby, Sleep

Sleep, baby, sleep,
   Our cottage vale is deep;
The little lamb is on the green
With woolly fleece so soft and clean –
   Sleep, baby, sleep.

Sleep, baby, sleep,
   Down where the woodbines creep;
Be always like the lamb so mild,
A kind and sweet and gentle child,
   Sleep, baby, sleep.

Bedtime

The Man in the Moon
Looked out of the moon,
Looked out of the moon and said,
" 'Tis time for all children on the earth
To think about getting to bed!"

Willie Winkie

Wee Willie Winkie runs through the town,
Upstairs and downstairs in his nightgown,
Rapping at the window, crying through the lock,
Are all the children in their beds, it's past eight o'clock?

To Bed

To bed, to bed,
Says Sleepyhead;
Tarry a while, says Slow;
Put on the pan,
Says Greedy Nan,
We'll sup before we go.

Baby Bunting

Bye, baby bunting,
Daddy's gone a-hunting,
Gone to get a rabbit skin
To wrap the baby bunting in.

Hush, Little Baby

Hush, little baby, don't say a word,
Papa's going to buy you a mockingbird.

If that mockingbird won't sing,
Papa's going to buy you a diamond ring.

If the diamond ring turns to brass,
Papa's going to buy you a looking glass.

If the looking glass gets broke,
Papa's going to buy you a billy goat.

If that billy goat runs away,
Papa's going to buy you another today.

Star Light

Star light, star bright,
First star I see tonight,
I wish I may, I wish I might,
Have the wish I wish tonight.

Twinkle, Twinkle

Twinkle, twinkle, little star,
How I wonder what you are!
Up above the world so high,
Like a diamond in the sky.

Niddledy,
Noddledy

Niddledy, noddledy
To and fro,
Tired and sleepy,
To bed we go,

Jump into bed,
Switch off the light,
Head on the pillow,
Shut your eyes tight.

Hush-a-Bye

Hush-a-bye, baby, on the treetop,
When the wind blows, the cradle will rock;
When the bough breaks, the cradle will fall;
Down will come baby, cradle, and all.

A Prayer

Send Daddy home
With a fiddle and a drum,
A pocket full of spices,
An apple and a plum.

Hush, My Baby

Hush, my baby, do not cry,
Papa's coming by and by;
When he comes he'll come in a gig,
Hi cockalorum, jig, jig, jig.

Hush Thee

Hush thee, my baby,
Lie still with thy daddy,
Thy mammy has gone to the mill,
To get some meal
To bake a cake,
So pray, my dear baby, lie still.

To Market

To market, to market, to buy a fat pig,
Home again, home again, jiggety-jig;

To market, to market, to buy a fat hog,
Home again, home again, jiggety-jog.

Pat-a-Cake

Pat-a-cake, pat-a-cake, baker's man,
Bake me a cake as fast as you can;
Pat it and prick it, and mark it with B,
Put it in the oven for Baby and me.

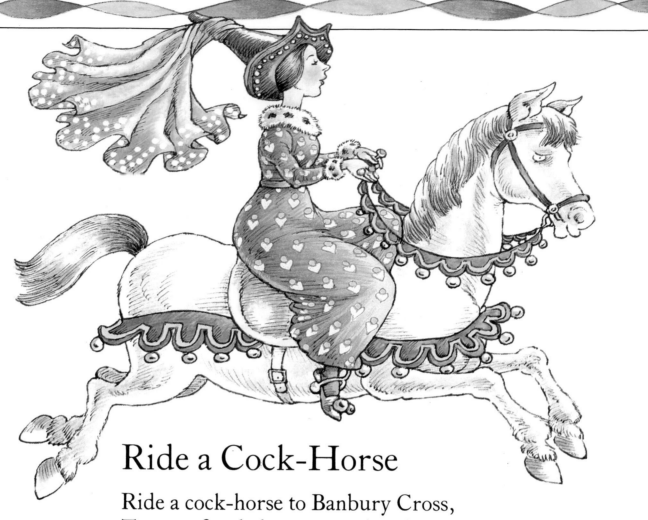

Ride a Cock-Horse

Ride a cock-horse to Banbury Cross,
To see a fine lady upon a white horse;
Rings on her fingers and bells on her toes,
She shall have music wherever she goes.

The Mischievous Raven

A farmer went trotting upon his gray mare,
    Bumpety, bumpety, bump!
With his daughter behind him so rosy and fair,
    Lumpety, lumpety, lump!

A raven cried, Croak! and they all tumbled down,
    Bumpety, bumpety, bump!
The mare broke her knees and the farmer his crown,
    Lumpety, lumpety, lump!

The mischievous raven flew laughing away,
    Bumpety, bumpety, bump!
And vowed he would serve them the same the next day,
    Lumpety, lumpety, lump!

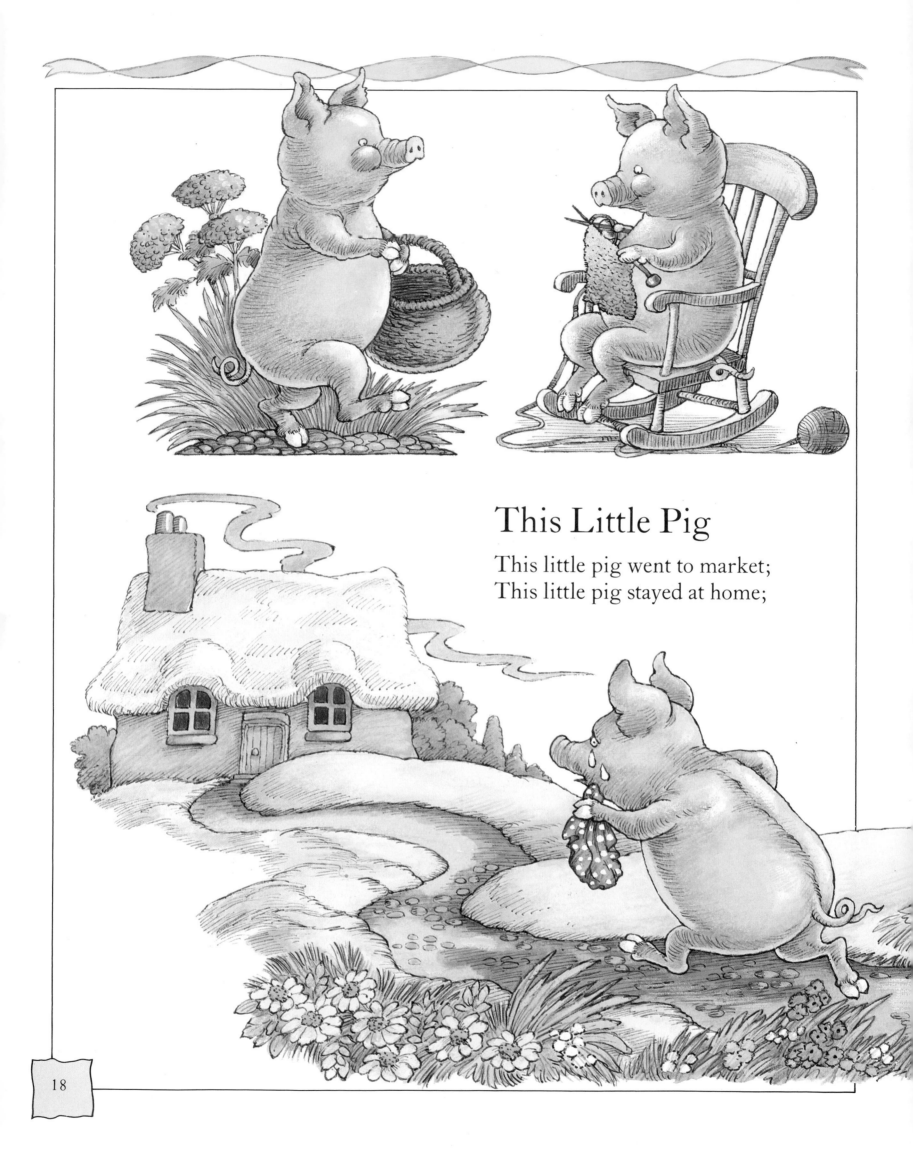

This Little Pig

This little pig went to market;
This little pig stayed at home;

This little pig had roast beef;
This little pig had none;
And this little pig cried, Wee-wee-wee!
    All the way home.

Humpty Dumpty

Humpty Dumpty sat on a wall,
Humpty Dumpty had a great fall;
   All the King's horses,
    And all the King's men,
Couldn't put Humpty together again.

The Little Nut Tree

I had a little nut tree,
    Nothing would it bear
But a silver nutmeg
    And a golden pear.
The king of Spain's daughter
    Came to visit me,
All for the sake
    Of my little nut tree.

Jack Sprat

Jack Sprat could eat no fat,
    His wife could eat no lean,
And so between them both, you see,
    They licked the platter clean.

Jack Horner

Little Jack Horner
Sat in the corner,
Eating his Christmas pie;
He put in his thumb,
And pulled out a plum,
And said, "What a good boy am I!"

Tom, Tom

Tom, Tom, the piper's son,
Stole a pig and away did run;
    The pig was eat,
    And Tom was beat,
And Tom went howling
    down the street.

Pease Pudding

Pease pudding hot,
Pease pudding cold,
Pease pudding in the pot,
Nine days old.
Some like it hot,
Some like it cold,
Some like it in the pot,
Nine days old.

Polly

Polly put the kettle on,
Polly put the kettle on,
Polly put the kettle on,
    We'll all have tea.

Sukey take it off again,
Sukey take it off again,
Sukey take it off again,
    They've all gone away.

Hot Cross Buns

Hot cross buns! Hot cross buns!
One a penny, two a penny,
Hot cross buns!
If you have no daughters
Give them to your sons;
One a penny, two a penny
Hot cross buns.

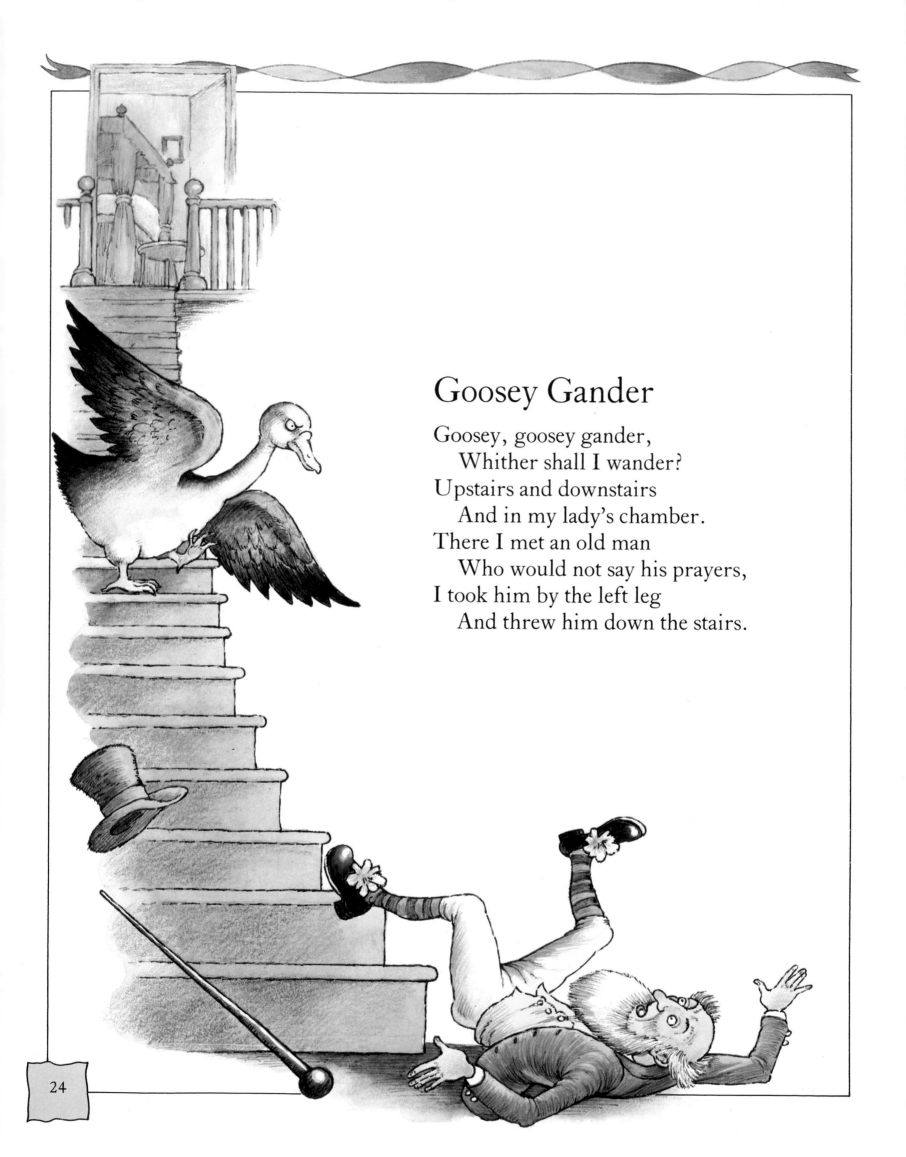

Goosey Gander

Goosey, goosey gander,
    Whither shall I wander?
Upstairs and downstairs
    And in my lady's chamber.
There I met an old man
    Who would not say his prayers,
I took him by the left leg
    And threw him down the stairs.

24

Cock a Doodle Doo

Cock a doodle doo!
My dame has lost her shoe,
My master's lost his fiddling stick
And knows not what to do.

Cock a doodle doo!
What is my dame to do?
Till master finds his fiddling stick
She'll dance without her shoe.

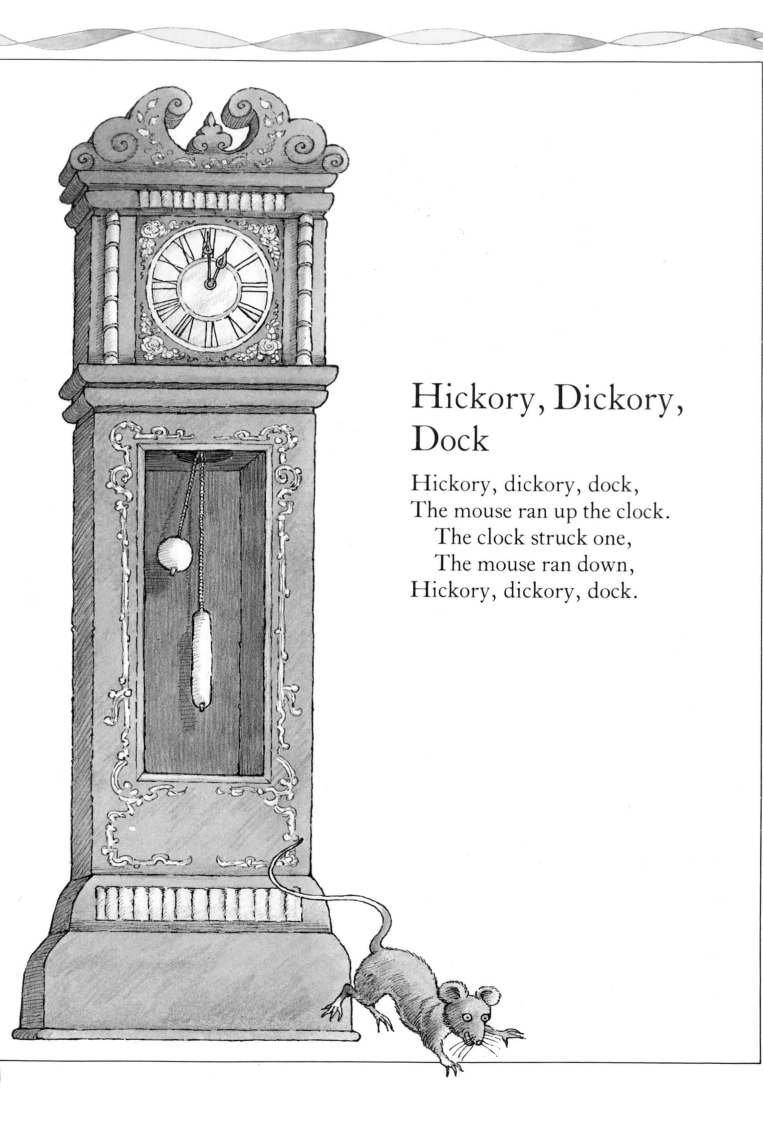

Hickory, Dickory, Dock

Hickory, dickory, dock,
The mouse ran up the clock.
The clock struck one,
The mouse ran down,
Hickory, dickory, dock.

Three Blind Mice

Three blind mice, see how they run!
They all ran after the farmer's wife,
Who cut off their tails with a carving knife,
Did you ever see such a thing in your life,
    As three blind mice?

My Black Hen

Hickety, pickety, my black hen,
She lays eggs for gentlemen;
Sometimes one, and sometimes ten,
Hickety, pickety, my black hen.

Lavender's Blue

Lavender's blue, dilly, dilly,
    Lavender's green,
When I am king, dilly, dilly,
    You shall be queen.

Call up your men, dilly, dilly,
    Set them to work,
Some to the plow, dilly, dilly,
    Some to the cart.

Some to make hay, dilly, dilly,
    Some to thresh corn,
Whilst you and I, dilly, dilly,
    Keep ourselves warm.

Contrary Mary

Mary, Mary, quite contrary,
    How does your garden grow?
With silver bells and cockle shells,
    And pretty maids all in a row.

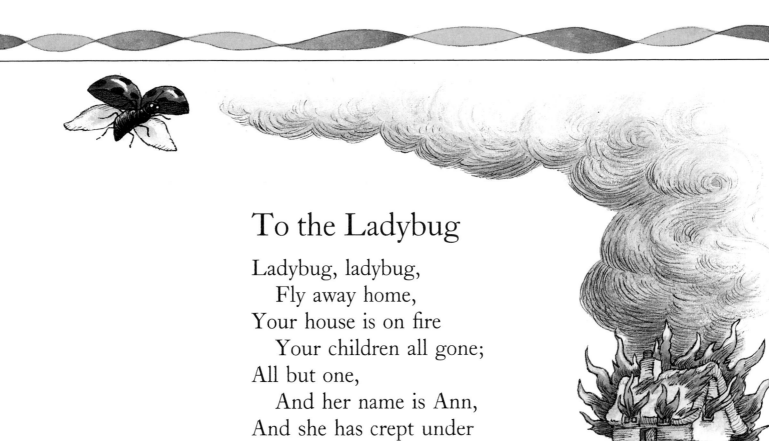

To the Ladybug

Ladybug, ladybug,
　Fly away home,
Your house is on fire
　Your children all gone;
All but one,
　And her name is Ann,
And she has crept under
　The warming pan.

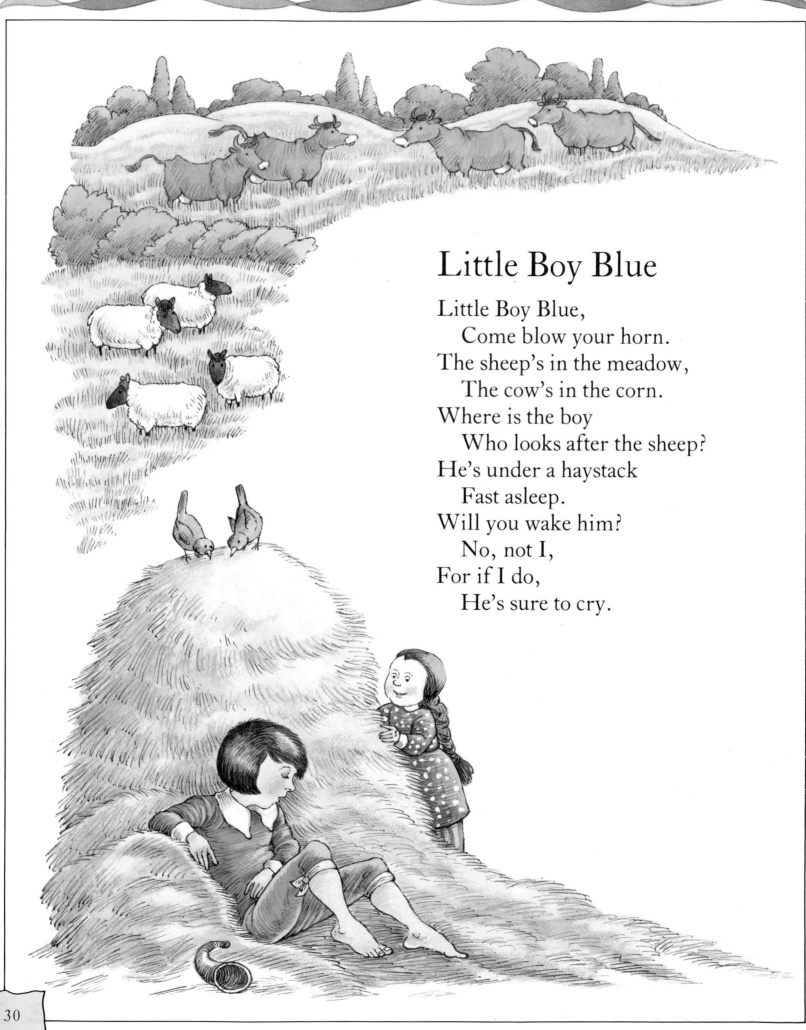

Little Boy Blue

Little Boy Blue,
　　Come blow your horn.
The sheep's in the meadow,
　　The cow's in the corn.
Where is the boy
　　Who looks after the sheep?
He's under a haystack
　　Fast asleep.
Will you wake him?
　　No, not I,
For if I do,
　　He's sure to cry.

Davy Dumpling

Davy Davy Dumpling,
Boil him in the pot;
Sugar him and butter him,
And eat him while he's hot.

Baa, Baa, Black Sheep

Baa, baa, black sheep,
    Have you any wool?
Yes, sir, yes, sir,
    Three bags full;
One for the master,
    And one for the dame,
And one for the little boy
    Who lives down the lane.

The Bells of London

Oranges and lemons,
Say the bells of St. Clement's.

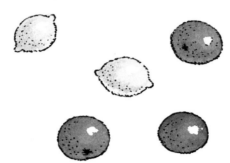

You owe me five farthings,
Say the bells of St. Martin's.

When will you pay me?
Say the bells of Old Bailey.

When I grow rich,
Say the bells of Shoreditch.

When will that be?
Say the bells of Stepney.

I'm sure I don't know,
Says the Great Bell of Bow.

Here comes the candle,
to light you to bed,
Here comes the chopper,
to chop off your head.

Ding, Dong, Bell

Ding, dong, bell,
Pussy's in the well.
Who put her in?
Little Johnny Green.
Who pulled her out?
Little Tommy Stout.
What a naughty boy was that
To try to drown poor pussycat,
Who never did him any harm,
But killed the mice in his father's barn.

Pop Goes the Weasel!

Up and down the City Road,
   In and out the Eagle,
That's the way the money goes,
   Pop goes the weasel!

Half a pound of tuppenny rice,
   Half a pound of treacle,
Mix it up and make it nice,
   Pop goes the weasel!

Every night when I go out
   The monkey's on the table;
Take a stick and knock it off,
   Pop goes the weasel!

Yankee Doodle

Yankee Doodle came to town,
   Riding on a pony,
He stuck a feather in his cap,
   And called it macaroni.

Sing a Song of Sixpence

Sing a song of sixpence,
    A pocket full of rye;
Four-and-twenty blackbirds,
    Baked in a pie.

When the pie was opened,
    The birds began to sing;
Was not that a dainty dish,
    To set before the king?

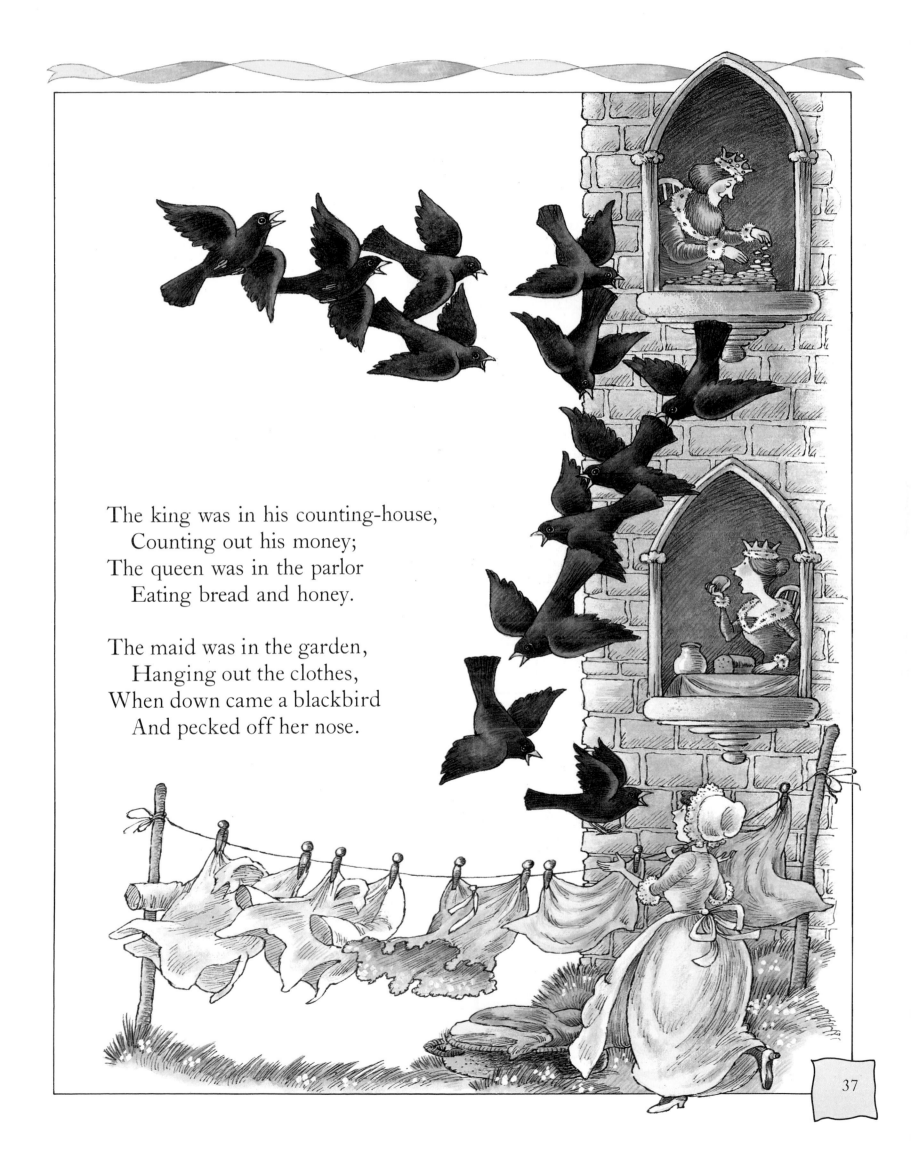

The king was in his counting-house,
  Counting out his money;
The queen was in the parlor
  Eating bread and honey.

The maid was in the garden,
  Hanging out the clothes,
When down came a blackbird
  And pecked off her nose.

Bobby Shaftoe

Bobby Shaftoe's gone to sea,
Silver buckles on his knee;
He'll come back and marry me,
   Bonny Bobby Shaftoe.

Bobby Shaftoe's bright and fair,
Combing down his yellow hair,
He's my love for evermore,
   Bonny Bobby Shaftoe.

I Saw a Ship A-Sailing

I saw a ship a-sailing,
   A-sailing on the sea,
And oh, but it was laden
   With pretty things for thee!

There were comfits in the cabin,
   And apples in the hold;
The sails were made of silk,
   And the masts were made of gold.

The four-and-twenty sailors,
   That stood between the decks,
Were four-and-twenty white mice
   With chains about their necks.

The captain was a duck
   With a packet on his back,
And when the ship began to move
   The captain said, "Quack! Quack!"

The Cat and the Fiddle

Hey diddle, diddle,
The cat and the fiddle,
The cow jumped over the moon;
The little dog laughed
To see such sport,
And the dish ran away with the spoon.

The Mulberry Bush

Here we go 'round the mulberry bush,
The mulberry bush, the mulberry bush,
Here we go 'round the mulberry bush,
On a cold and frosty morning.

See-Saw, Margery Daw

See-saw, Margery Daw,
Johnny shall have a new master;
He shall have but a penny a day,
Because he can't work any faster.

Jack

Jack be nimble,
   Jack be quick,
Jack jump over
   The candlestick.

Ring-a-Ring O' Roses

Ring-a-ring o' roses,
A pocket full of posies,
   Ashes! Ashes!
We all fall down.

Old King Cole

Old King Cole was a merry old soul,
And a merry old soul was he;
He called for his pipe and he called for his bowl,
And he called for his fiddlers three.

Every fiddler had a fiddle,
And a very fine fiddle had he;
Oh, there's none so rare as can compare
With King Cole and his fiddlers three.

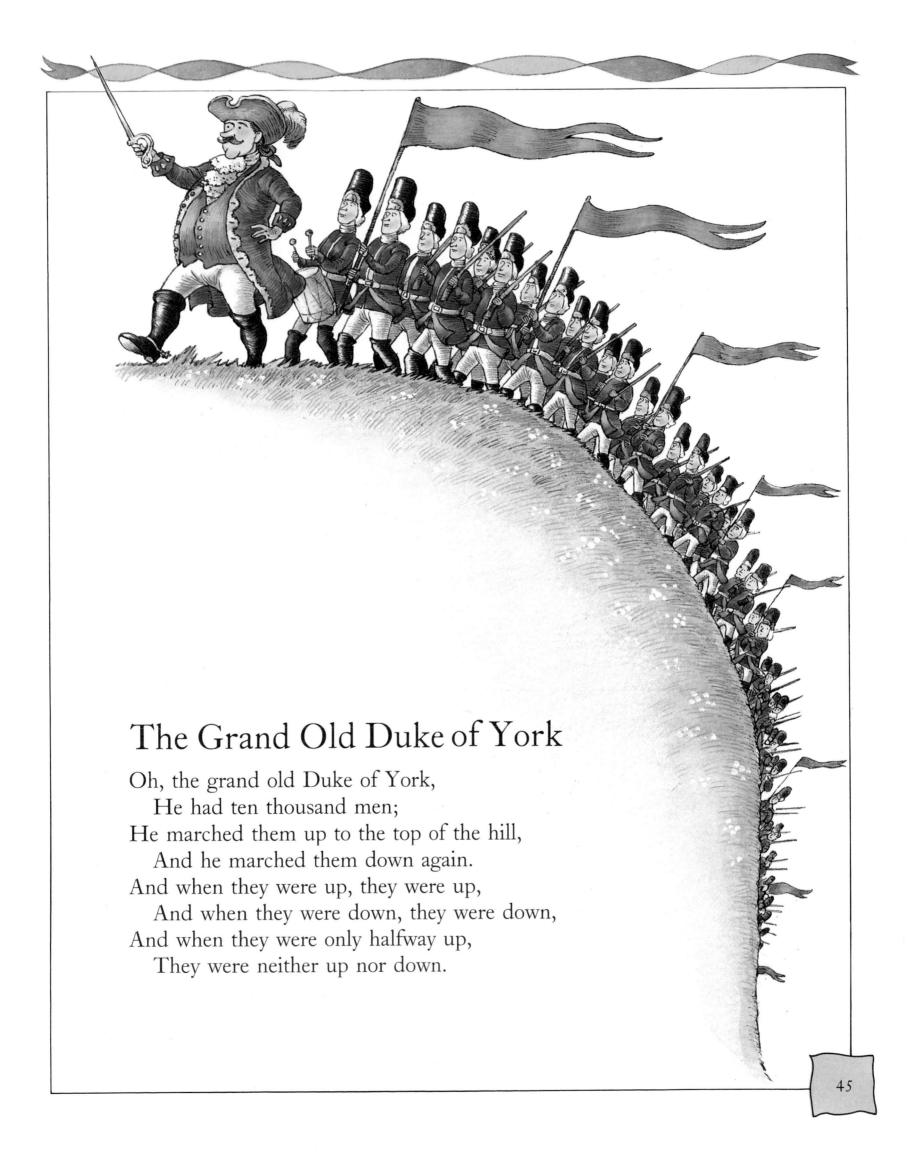

The Grand Old Duke of York

Oh, the grand old Duke of York,
　　He had ten thousand men;
He marched them up to the top of the hill,
　　And he marched them down again.
And when they were up, they were up,
　　And when they were down, they were down,
And when they were only halfway up,
　　They were neither up nor down.

Girls and Boys
Come Out to Play

Girls and boys come out to play,
The moon doth shine as bright as day.
Leave your supper and leave your sleep,
And come with your playfellows into the street.
Come with a whoop and come with a call,
Come with a good will or not at all.
Up the ladder and down the wall,
A half-penny loaf will serve us all;
You find milk, and I'll find flour,
And we'll have a pudding in half an hour.

Three Men in a Tub

Rub-a-dub-dub,
Three men in a tub,
And how do you think they got there?
The butcher, the baker,
The candlestick maker,
They all jumped out of a rotten potato,
'Twas enough to make a man stare.

To the Rain

Rain, rain, go away,
Come again another day,
Little Johnny wants to play.
Rain, rain, go to Spain,
Never show your face again.

It's Raining

It's raining, it's pouring,
The old man is snoring;
He went to bed
And bumped his head
And couldn't get up in
    the morning.

Jingle Bells

Jingle, bells! Jingle, bells!
    Jingle all the way;
Oh, what fun it is to ride
    In a one-horse open sleigh.

Christmas is Coming

Christmas is coming,
The geese are getting fat,
Please to put a penny
In the old man's hat.
If you haven't got a penny,
A ha'penny will do;
If you haven't got a ha'penny,
Then God bless you!

Eentsy Weentsy

Eentsy Weentsy spider,
    Climbed up the water spout;
Down came the rain
    And washed the spider out;
Out came the sunshine
    And dried up all the rain;
Eentsy Weentsy spider,
    Climbed up the spout again.

Alphabet Pie

A was an
Apple pie

B
Bit it

C
Cut it

D
Dealt it

E
Enjoyed it

F
Fought for it

G
Got it

H
Had it

I
Inspected it

J
Jumped for it

K
Kept it

L
Longed for it

M
Mourned for it

N
Nodded at it

O
Opened it

P
Peeped in it

Q
Quartered it

R
Ran for it

S
Stole it

T
Took it

U
Upset it

V
Viewed it

W
Wanted it

XYZ & ampersand
All wished for
a piece in hand

A Week of Birthdays

Monday's child is fair of face,
Tuesday's child is full of grace,
Wednesday's child is full of woe,
Thursday's child has far to go,
Friday's child is loving and giving,
Saturday's child works hard for its living,
And the child that's born on the Sabbath day
Is bonny and blithe, and good and gay.

Solomon Grundy

Solomon Grundy,
Born on a Monday,
Christened on Tuesday,
Married on Wednesday,
Took ill on Thursday,
Worse on Friday,
Died on Saturday,
Buried on Sunday.
This is the end
Of Solomon Grundy.

The Cuckoo

Cuckoo, cuckoo, what do you do?
In April I open my bill;
In May I sing all day;
In June I change my tune;
In July I prepare to fly;
In August away I must.

Days in the Months

Thirty days hath September,
April, June, and November;
All the rest have thirty-one.
Excepting February alone,
And that has twenty-eight days clear
And twenty-nine in each leap year.

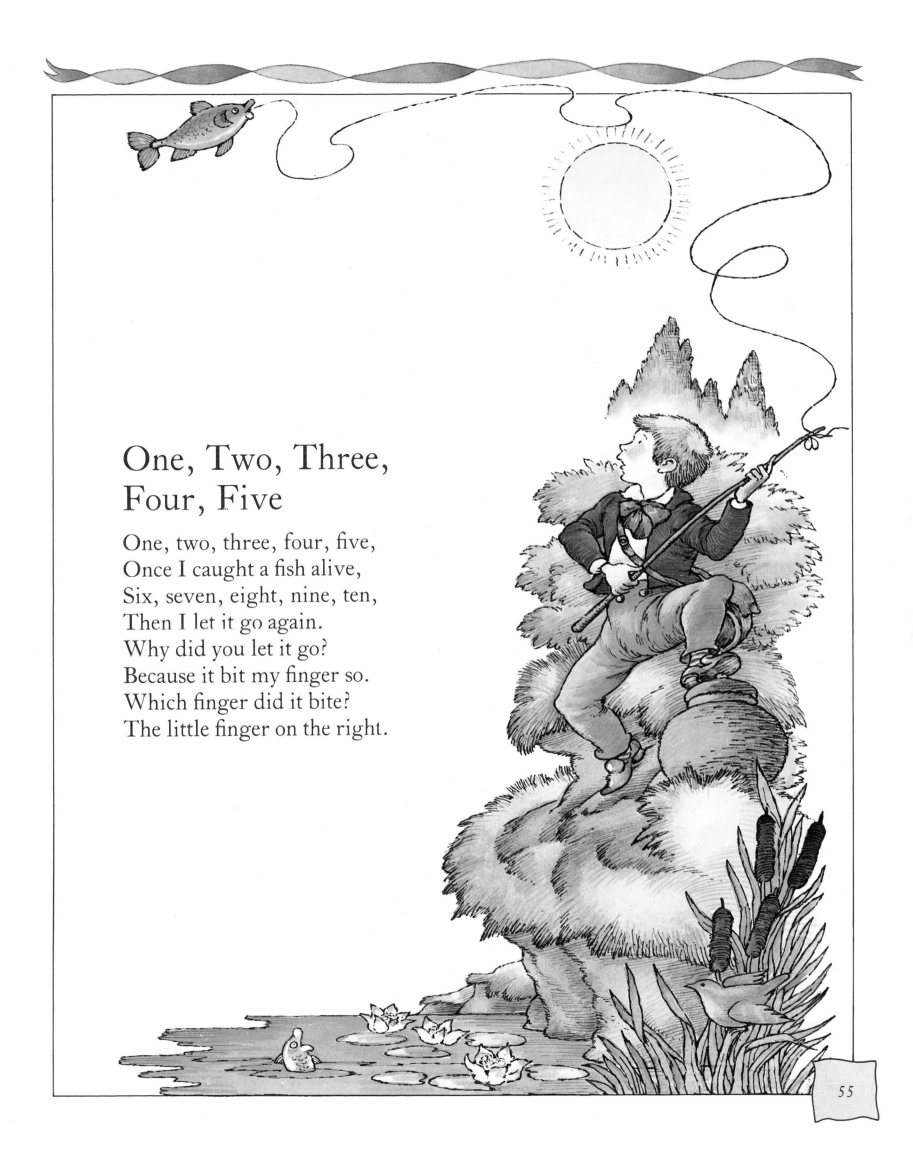

One, Two, Three, Four, Five

One, two, three, four, five,
Once I caught a fish alive,
Six, seven, eight, nine, ten,
Then I let it go again.
Why did you let it go?
Because it bit my finger so.
Which finger did it bite?
The little finger on the right.

One, Two

1, 2,
Buckle my shoe;

3, 4,
Knock at the door;

5, 6,
Pick up sticks;

7, 8,
Lay them straight;

9, 10,
A big fat hen;

11, 12,
Dig and delve;

13, 14,
Maids a-courting;

15, 16,
Maids in the kitchen;

17, 18,
Maids a-waiting;

19, 20,
My plate's empty.

To the Magpie

Magpie, magpie, flutter and flee,
Turn up your tail and good luck come to me.
One for sorrow, two for joy,
Three for a girl, four for a boy,
Five for silver, six for gold,
Seven for a secret ne'er to be told.

Going to St. Ives

As I was going to St. Ives,
I met a man with seven wives;
Each wife had seven sacks,
Each sack had seven cats,
Each cat had seven kits:
Kits, cats, sacks, and wives,
How many were there going to St. Ives?
                    (*One or none*)

Mary's Lamb

Mary had a little lamb,
    Its fleece was white as snow;
And everywhere that Mary went
    The lamb was sure to go.

It followed her to school one day,
    That was against the rule;
It made the children laugh and play
    To see a lamb at school.

And so the teacher turned it out,
    But still it lingered near,
And waited patiently about
    Till Mary did appear.

Why does the lamb love Mary so?
    The eager children cry;
Why, Mary loves the lamb, you know,
    The teacher did reply.

Old Mother Hubbard

Old Mother Hubbard
Went to her cupboard,
To fetch her poor dog a bone;
But when she got there
The cupboard was bare
And so the poor dog had none.

She went to the baker's
To buy him some bread;
But when she came back
The poor dog was dead.

She went to the joiner's
To buy him a coffin;
But when she came back
The poor dog was laughing.

She took a clean dish
   To get him some tripe;
But when she came back
   He was smoking a pipe.

She went to the fishmonger's
   To buy him some fish;
But when she came back
   He was licking the dish.

She went to the tavern
   For white wine and red;
But when she came back
   The dog stood on his head.

She went to the fruiterer's
   To buy him some fruit;
But when she came back
   He was playing the flute.

She went to the tailor's
  To buy him a coat;
But when she came back
  He was riding a goat.

She went to the hatter's
  To buy him a hat;
But when she came back
  He was feeding the cat.

She went to the barber's
  To buy him a wig;
But when she came back
  He was dancing a jig.

She went to the cobbler's
  To buy him some shoes;
But when she came back
  He was reading the news.

She went to the seamstress
    To buy him some linen;
But when she came back
    The dog was a-spinning.

She went to the hosier's
    To buy him some hose;
But when she came back
    He was dressed in his clothes.

The dame made a curtsey,
    The dog made a bow;
The dame said, "Your servant,"
    The dog said, "Bow-wow."

Jack and Jill

Jack and Jill
Went up the hill,
To fetch a pail of water;
Jack fell down,
And broke his crown,
And Jill came tumbling after.

Then up Jack got,
And home did trot,
As fast as he could caper;
To old Dame Dob,
Who patched his knob
With vinegar and brown paper.

When Jill came in,
How she did grin
To see Jack's paper plaster;
His mother, vexed,
Did whip her next,
For laughing at Jack's disaster.

Now Jack did laugh
And Jill did cry,
But her tears did soon abate;
Then Jill did say,
That they should play
A seesaw across the gate.

The Crooked Man

There was a crooked man,
   And he walked a crooked mile,
He found a crooked sixpence
   Against a crooked stile;
He bought a crooked cat,
   Which caught a crooked mouse,
And they all lived together
   In a little crooked house.

Polly Flinders

Little Polly Flinders
Sat amongst the cinders,
Warming her pretty little toes;
Her mother came and caught her,
And whipped her little daughter
For spoiling her nice new clothes.

Old Mother Shuttle

Old Mother Shuttle,
   Lived in a coal-scuttle
Along with her dog and her cat;
   What they ate I can't tell,
   But 'tis known very well
That not one of the party was fat.

Old Mother Shuttle
   Scoured out her coal-scuttle,
And washed both her dog and her cat;
   The cat scratched her nose,
   So they came to hard blows,
And who was the gainer by that?

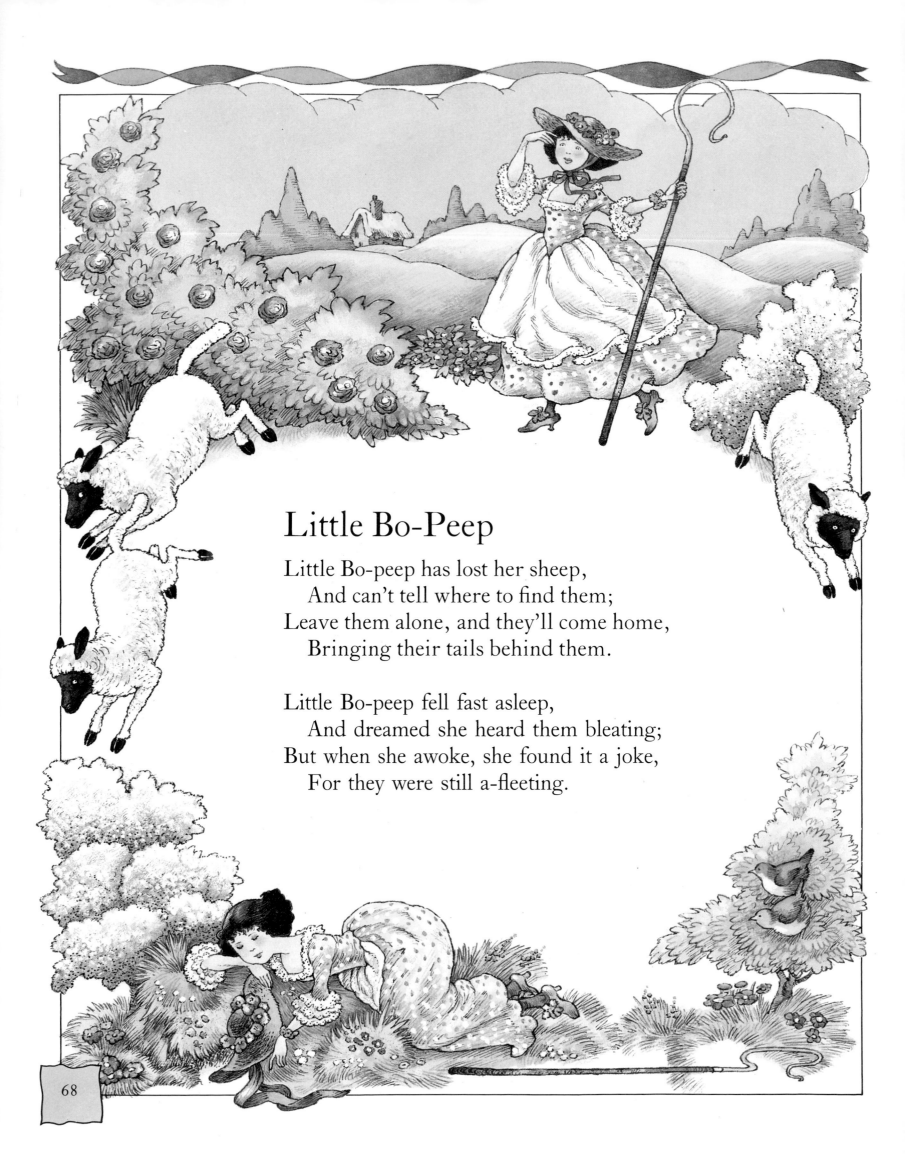

Little Bo-Peep

Little Bo-peep has lost her sheep,
    And can't tell where to find them;
Leave them alone, and they'll come home,
    Bringing their tails behind them.

Little Bo-peep fell fast asleep,
    And dreamed she heard them bleating;
But when she awoke, she found it a joke,
    For they were still a-fleeting.

Then up she took her little crook,
    Determined for to find them;
She found them indeed, but it made her heart bleed
    For they'd left their tails behind them.

It happened one day, as Bo-peep did stray
    Into a meadow hard by,
There she espied their tails side by side,
    All hung on a tree to dry.

She heaved a sigh, and wiped her eye,
    And over the hillocks went rambling,
And tried what she could as a shepherdess should,
    To tack each again to its lambkin.

Old Mother Goose

Old Mother Goose,
    When she wanted to wander,
Would ride through the air
    On a very fine gander.

Mother Goose had a house,
    'Twas built in a wood,
Where an owl at the door
    For sentinel stood.

She had a son Jack,
    A plain-looking lad,
He was not very good,
    Nor yet very bad.

She sent him to market,
    A live goose he bought;
See, mother, says he,
    I have not been for nought.

Jack's goose and her gander
    Grew very fond;
They'd both eat together,
    Or swim in the pond.

Jack found one fine morning,
    As I have been told,
His goose had laid him
    An egg of pure gold.

Jack ran to his mother
    The news for to tell,
She called him a good boy,
    And said it was well.

Jack sold his gold egg
    To a merchant untrue,
Who cheated him out of
    A half of his due.

Then Jack went a-courting
   A lady so gay,
As fair as the lily,
   And sweet as the May.

The merchant and squire
   Soon came at his back,
And began to belabor
   The sides of poor Jack.

Then old Mother Goose
   That instant came in,
And turned her son Jack
   Into famed Harlequin.

The Man with Nought

There was a man and he had nought,
    And robbers came to rob him;
He crept up to the chimney pot,
    And then they thought they had him.

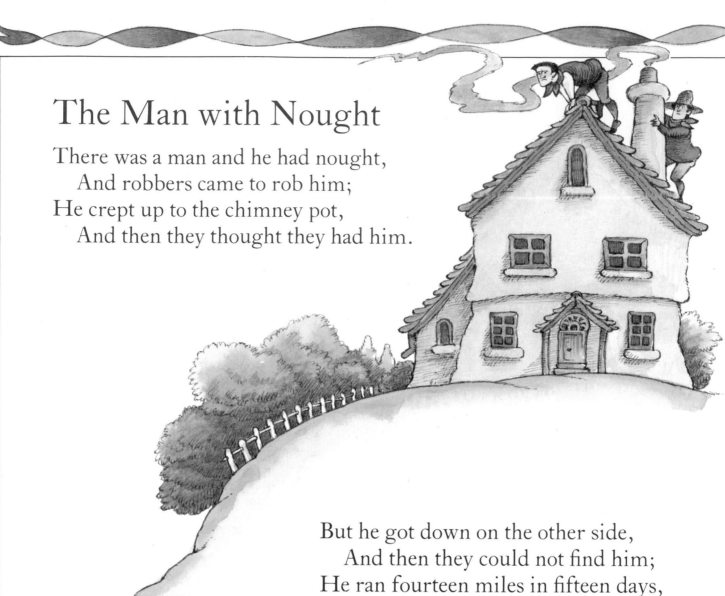

But he got down on the other side,
    And then they could not find him;
He ran fourteen miles in fifteen days,
    And never looked behind him.

The Jolly Miller

There was a jolly miller once,
    Lived on the river Dee;
He worked and sang from morn till night,
    No lark more blithe than he.
And this the burden of his song
    Forever used to be,
I care for nobody, no, not I,
    If nobody cares for me.

Little Miss Muffet

Little Miss Muffet
Sat on a tuffet,
Eating her curds and whey;
There came a big spider,
Who sat down beside her
And frightened Miss Muffet away.

Pussycat, Pussycat

Pussycat, pussycat,
    Where have you been?
I've been to London
    To look at the Queen.

Pussycat, pussycat,
    What did you there?
I frightened a little mouse
    Under her chair.

The Queen of Hearts

The Queen of Hearts
She made some tarts,
All on a summer's day;
The Knave of Hearts
He stole the tarts,
And took them clean away.

The King of Hearts
Called for the tarts,
And beat the knave full sore;
The Knave of Hearts
Brought back the tarts,
And vowed he'd steal no more.

Simple Simon

Simple Simon met a pieman,
    Going to the fair;
Says Simple Simon to the pieman,
    Let me taste your ware.

Says the pieman to Simple Simon,
    Show me first your penny;
Says Simple Simon to the pieman,
    Indeed I have not any.

Simple Simon went a-fishing,
  For to catch a whale;
All the water he had got
  Was in his mother's pail.

Simple Simon went to look
  If plums grew on a thistle;
He pricked his fingers very much,
  Which made poor Simon whistle.

He went for water in a sieve
  But soon it all ran through;
And now poor Simple Simon
  Bids you all adieu.

Three Little Kittens

Three little kittens
They lost their mittens,
    And they began to cry,
Oh, Mother dear,
We sadly fear
Our mittens we have lost.
What! lost your mittens,
You naughty kittens!
Then you shall have no pie.
    Mee-ow, mee-ow, mee-ow.
No, you shall have no pie.

The three little kittens
They found their mittens,
    And they began to cry,
Oh, Mother dear,
See here, see here,
Our mittens we have found.
Put on your mittens,
You silly kittens,
And you shall have some pie.
    Purr-r, purr-r, purr-r,
Oh, let us have some pie.

The three little kittens
Put on their mittens
    And soon ate up the pie;
Oh, Mother dear,
We greatly fear
Our mittens we have soiled.
What! soiled your mittens,
You naughty kittens!
Then they began to sigh,
    Mee-ow, mee-ow, mee-ow,
Then they began to sigh.

The three little kittens
They washed their mittens,
    And hung them out to dry;
Oh, Mother dear,
Do you not hear,
Our mittens we have washed.
What! washed your mittens,
You good little kittens,
But I smell a rat close by.
    Mee-ow, mee-ow, mee-ow,
We smell a rat close by.

The Old Woman in a Shoe

There was an old woman who lived in a shoe;
She had so many children she didn't know what to do.
She gave them some broth without any bread;
Then whipped them all soundly and put them to bed.

Peter, Peter

Peter, Peter, pumpkin eater,
Had a wife and couldn't keep her;
He put her in a pumpkin shell,
And there he kept her very well.

The Pie

Who made the pie?
I did.

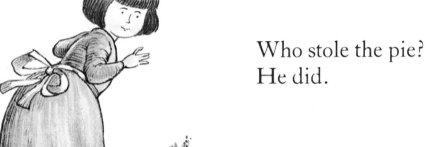

Who stole the pie?
He did.

Who found the pie?
She did.

Who cried for pie?
We all did.

Who ate the pie?
You did.

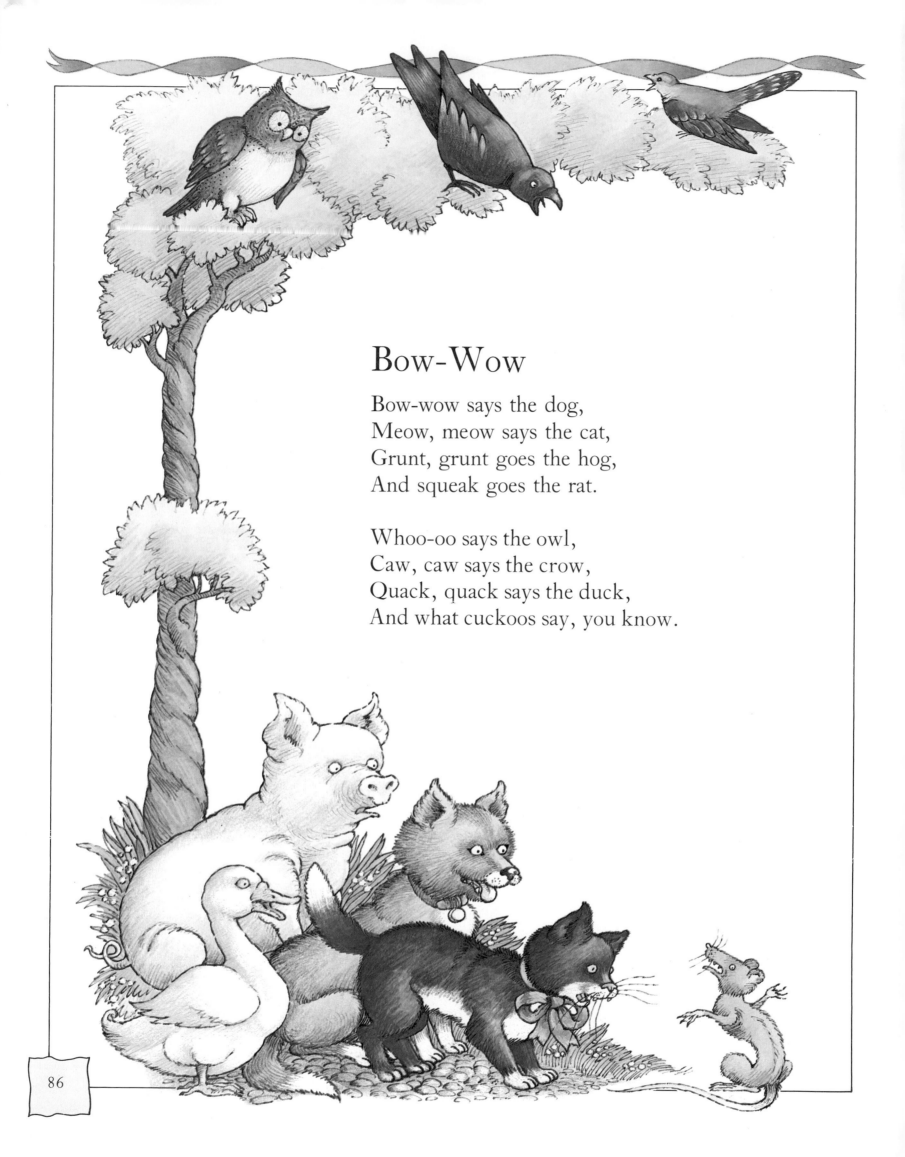

Bow-Wow

Bow-wow says the dog,
Meow, meow says the cat,
Grunt, grunt goes the hog,
And squeak goes the rat.

Whoo-oo says the owl,
Caw, caw says the crow,
Quack, quack says the duck,
And what cuckoos say, you know.

The Donkey

If I had a donkey that wouldn't go,
Would I beat him? Oh no, no.
I'd put him in the barn and give him some corn.
The best little donkey that ever was born.

Old Woman

There was an old woman
  Lived under a hill,
And if she's not gone
  She lives there still.

Roses Are Red

Roses are red,
Violets are blue,
Sugar is sweet
And so are you.

On Saturday Night

On Saturday night I lost my wife,
And where do you think I found her?
Up in the moon, singing a tune,
And all the stars around her.

The Milkmaid

Little maid, pretty maid,
   Whither goest thou?
Down to the meadow
   To milk my cow.
Shall I go with thee?
   No, not now.
When I send for thee,
   Then come thou.

Three Young Rats

Three young rats with black felt hats,
Three young ducks with new straw flats,
Three young dogs with curling tails,
Three young cats with demi-veils,
Went out to walk with two young pigs
In satin vests and sorrel wigs;
But suddenly it chanced to rain
And so they all went home again.

The Kilkenny Cats

There were once two cats of Kilkenny,
Each thought there was one cat too many;
So they fought and they fit,
And they scratched and they bit,
   Till, excepting their nails,
   And the tips of their tails,
Instead of two cats, there weren't any.

Corporal Bull

Here's Corporal Bull
A strong hearty fellow,
Who not used to fighting
Set up a loud bellow.

Little Tommy Tittlemouse

Little Tommy Tittlemouse
Lived in a little house;
He caught fishes
In other men's ditches.

Lucy Locket

Lucy Locket lost her pocket,
    Kitty Fisher found it;
Not a penny was there in it,
    Only ribbon 'round it.

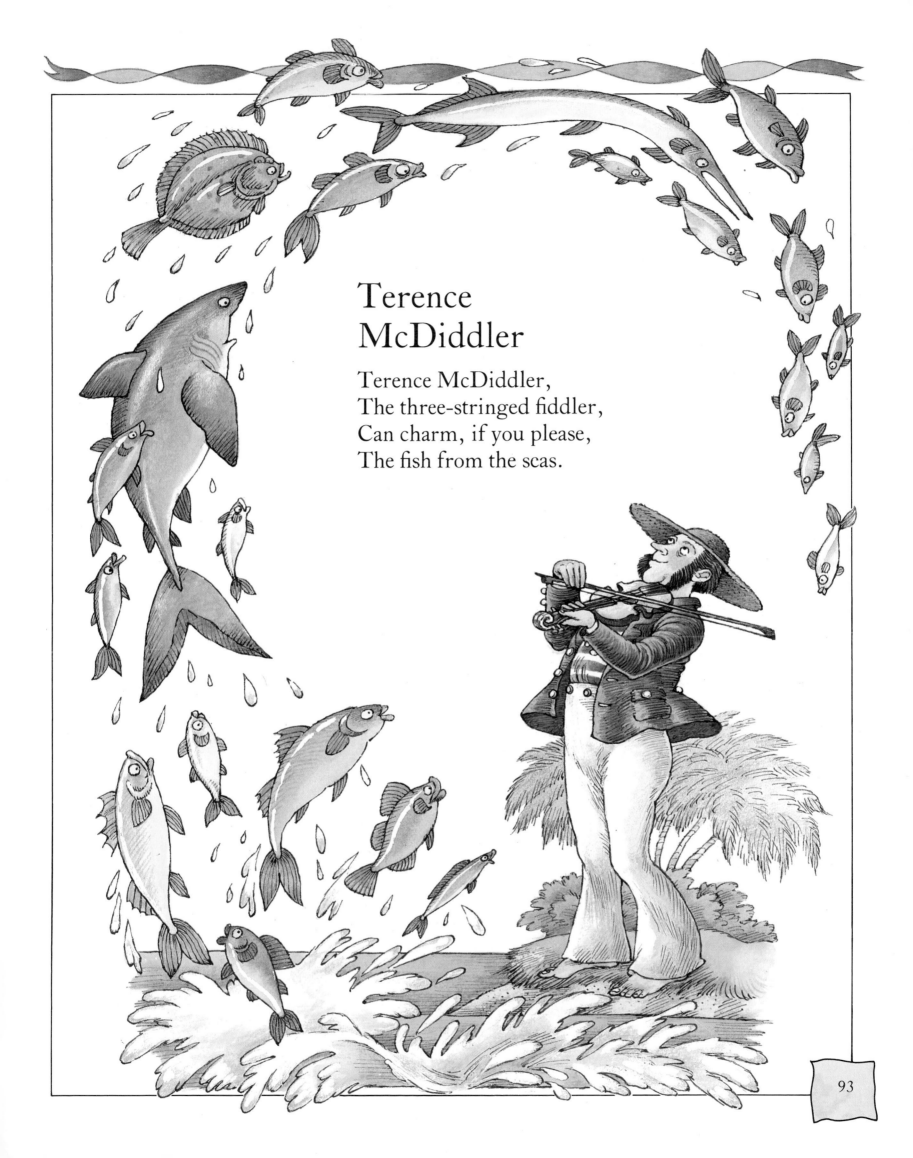

Terence McDiddler

Terence McDiddler,
The three-stringed fiddler,
Can charm, if you please,
The fish from the seas.

An Old Woman

There was an old woman tossed up in a basket,
Seventeen times as high as the moon;
And where was she going, I couldn't but ask it,
For in her hand she carried a broom.

Old woman, old woman, old woman, said I,
Where are you going to up so high?
To sweep the cobwebs off the sky!
Shall I go with you? Aye, by-and-by.

Bandy Legs

As I was going to sell my eggs
I met a man with bandy legs,
Bandy legs and crooked toes;
I tripped up his heels, and he fell on his nose.

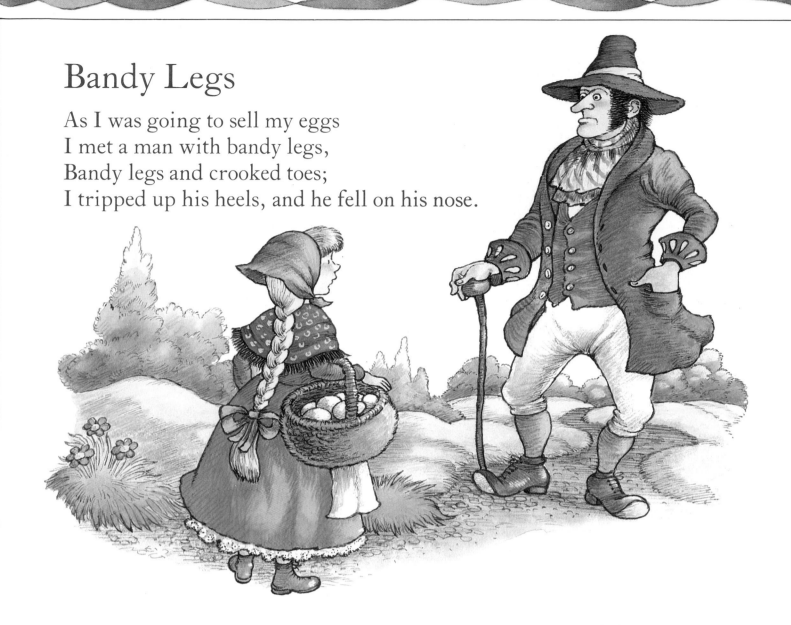

A Man in the Wilderness

A man in the wilderness asked me,
How many strawberries grow in the sea?
I answered him, as I thought good,
As many red herrings as swim in the wood.

To the Bat

Bat, bat, come under my hat,
　　And I'll give you a slice of bacon;
And when I bake, I'll give you a cake,
　　If I am not mistaken.

Higglety, Pigglety

Higglety, pigglety, pop!
The dog has eaten the mop;
　　The pig's in a hurry,
　　The cat's in a flurry,
Higglety, pigglety, pop!

The Flying Pig

Dickery, dickery, dare,
The pig flew up in the air;
The man in brown
Soon brought him down,
Dickery, dickery, dare.

Pussycat Mew

Pussycat mew jumped over a coal,
And in her best petticoat burned a great hole;
Pussycat mew shall have no more milk,
Until her best petticoat's mended with silk.

Hoddley, Poddley

Hoddley, poddley, puddle, and fogs,
Cats are to marry the poodle dogs;
Cats in blue jackets and dogs in red hats,
What will become of the mice and the rats?

Goose Feathers

Cackle, cackle, Mother Goose,
Have you any feathers loose?
Truly have I, pretty fellow,
Half enough to fill a pillow.
Here are quills, take one or two,
And down to make a bed for you.

To the Snail

Snail, snail, put out your horns,
And I'll give you bread and barley corns.

The Wind

When the wind is in the east,
'Tis neither good for man nor beast;
When the wind is in the north,
The skillful fisher goes not forth;
When the wind is in the south,
It blows the bait in the fishes' mouth;
When the wind is in the west,
Then 'tis at the very best.

One Misty, Moisty Morning

One misty, moisty morning,
    When cloudy was the weather,
There I met an old man
    Clothed all in leather.

He began to compliment,
    And I began to grin,
How do you do, and how do you do,
    And how do you do again?

The North Wind

The north wind doth blow,
And we shall have snow,
And what will poor Robin do then,
    Poor thing?
He'll sit in a barn,
And keep himself warm,
And hide his head under his wing,
    Poor thing.

The House that Jack Built

This is the house
that Jack built.

This is the malt
That lay in the house
that Jack built.

This is the rat,
That ate the malt
That lay in the house
that Jack built.

This is the dog,
That worried the cat,
That killed the rat,
That ate the malt
That lay in the house
that Jack built.

This is the cat,
That killed the rat,
That ate the malt
That lay in the house
that Jack built.

This is the cow
   with the crumpled horn,
That tossed the dog,
That worried the cat,
That killed the rat,
That ate the malt
That lay in the house
   that Jack built.

This is the maiden all forlorn,
That milked the cow
   with the crumpled horn,
That tossed the dog,
That worried the cat,
That killed the rat,
That ate the malt
That lay in the house
   that Jack built.

This is the man all tattered
    and torn,
That kissed the maiden
    all forlorn,
That milked the cow
    with the crumpled horn,
That tossed the dog,
That worried the cat,
That killed the rat,
That ate the malt
That lay in the house
    that Jack built.

This is the priest all shaven and shorn,
That married the man
    all tattered and torn,
That kissed the maiden
    all forlorn,
That milked the cow
    with the crumpled horn,
That tossed the dog,
That worried the cat,
That killed the rat,
That ate the malt
That lay in the house
    that Jack built.

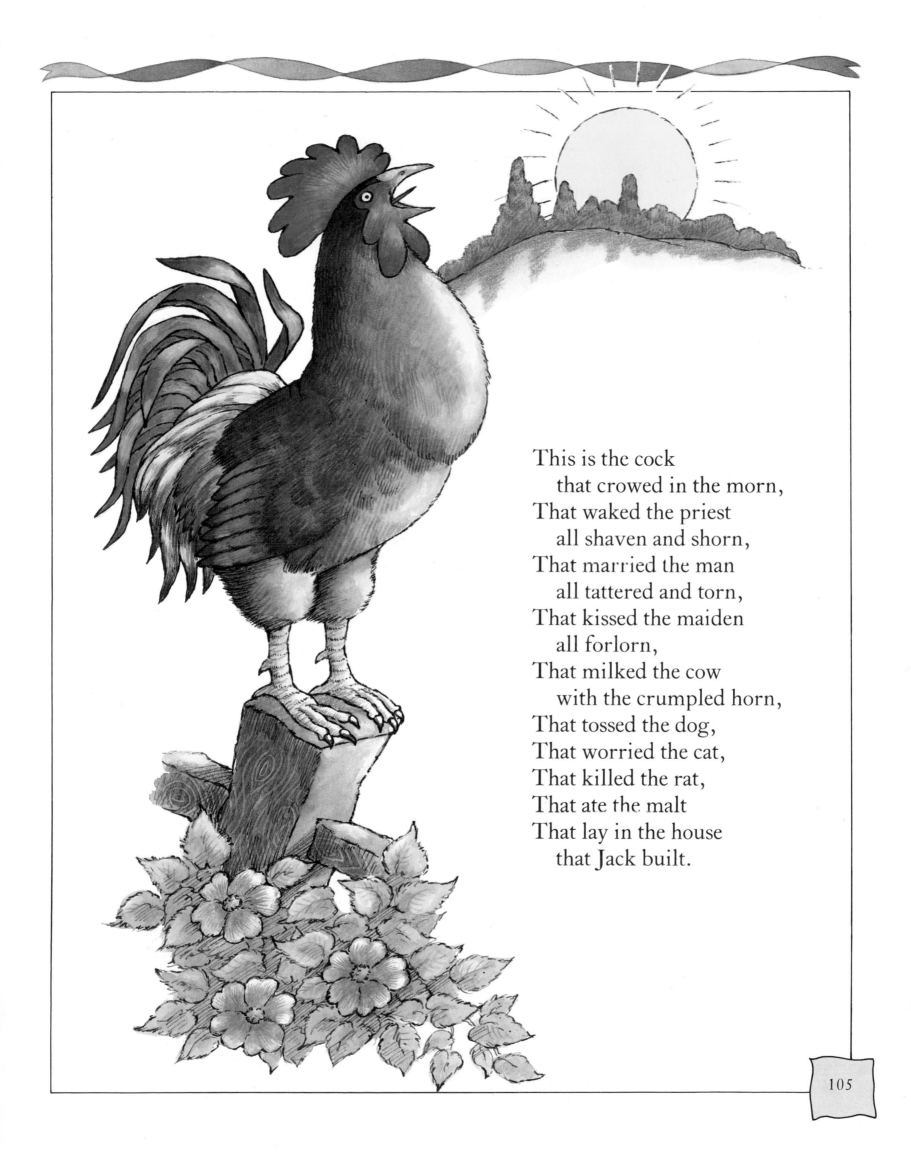

This is the cock
    that crowed in the morn,
That waked the priest
    all shaven and shorn,
That married the man
    all tattered and torn,
That kissed the maiden
    all forlorn,
That milked the cow
    with the crumpled horn,
That tossed the dog,
That worried the cat,
That killed the rat,
That ate the malt
That lay in the house
    that Jack built.

This is the farmer sowing his corn,
That kept the cock that crowed in the morn,
That waked the priest all shaven and shorn,
That married the man all tattered and torn,
That kissed the maiden all forlorn,
That milked the cow with
    the crumpled horn,
That tossed the dog,
That worried the cat,
That killed the rat,
That ate the malt
That lay in the house
    that Jack built.

This is the horse and the hound and the horn,
That belonged to the farmer sowing his corn,
That kept the cock that crowed in the morn,
That waked the priest all shaven and shorn,
That married the man all tattered and torn,
That kissed the maiden all forlorn,
            That milked the cow with
                the crumpled horn,
            That tossed the dog,
            That worried the cat,
            That killed the rat,
            That ate the malt
            That lay in the house
                that Jack built.

Jack-a-Nory

I'll tell you a story
About Jack-a-Nory,
And now my story's begun;
I'll tell you another
About Jack and his brother,
And now my story is done.

A Nail

For want of a nail
   the shoe was lost,
For want of a shoe
   the horse was lost,
For want of a horse
   the rider was lost,
For want of a rider
   the battle was lost,
For want of a battle
   the kingdom was lost,
And all for the want
   of a horseshoe nail.

The Key of the Kingdom

This is the key of the kingdom.
In that kingdom is a city,
In that city is a town,
In that town there is a street,
In that street there winds a lane,
In that lane there is a yard,
In that yard there is a house,
In that house there waits a room,
On that bed there is a basket,
    A basket of flowers.

Flowers in the basket,
Basket on the bed,
Bed in the chamber,
Chamber in the house,
House in the weedy yard,
Yard in the winding lane,
Lane in the broad street,
Street in the high town,
Town in the city,
City in the kingdom:
    This is the key of the kingdom.

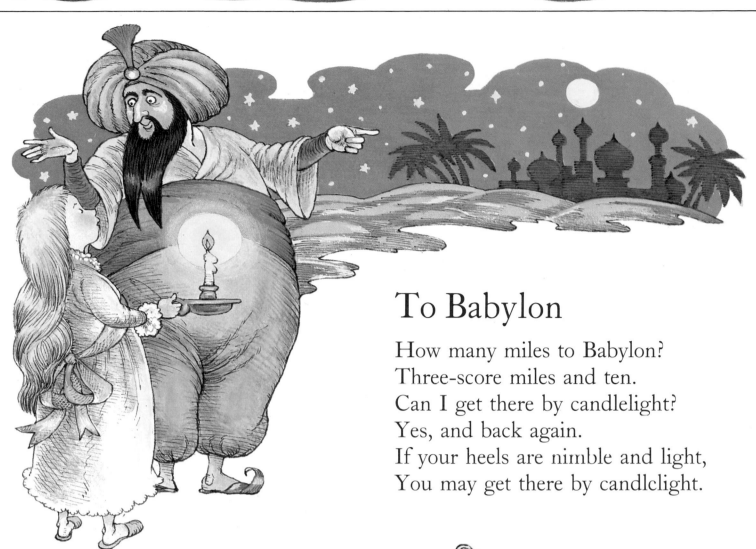

To Babylon

How many miles to Babylon?
Three-score miles and ten.
Can I get there by candlelight?
Yes, and back again.
If your heels are nimble and light,
You may get there by candlclight.

Ten O'Clock Scholar

A diller, a dollar,
A ten o'clock scholar,
What makes you come so soon?
You used to come at ten o'clock,
But now you come at noon.

Where, Oh Where

Oh where, oh where has my little dog gone?
 Oh where, oh where can he be?
With his ears cut short and his tail cut long,
 Oh where, oh where is he?

The Beggars

Hark, hark, the dogs do bark,
 The beggars are coming to town;
Some in rags and some in jags,
 And one in a velvet gown.

Six Little Mice

Six little mice sat down to spin;
Pussy passed by and she peeped in.
What are you doing, my little men?
Weaving coats for gentlemen.
Shall I come in and cut off your threads?
No, no, Mistress Pussy, you'd bite off our heads.
Oh, no, I'll not; I'll help you to spin.
That may be so, but you don't come in.

Jeremiah

Jeremiah, blow the fire,
    Puff, puff, puff!
First you blow it gently,
    Then you blow it rough.

Diddle, Diddle, Dumpling

Diddle, diddle, dumpling, my son John,
Went to bed with his trousers on;
One shoe off, and one shoe on,
Diddle, diddle, dumpling, my son John.

Doctor Foster

Doctor Foster went to Gloucester
In a shower of rain;
He stepped in a puddle,
Right up to his middle,
And never went there again.

Queen Caroline

Queen, Queen Caroline,
Washed her hair in turpentine,
Turpentine to make it shine,
Queen, Queen Caroline.

A Man of Thessaly

There was a man of Thessaly
  And he was wondrous wise,
He jumped into a bramble bush
  And scratched out both his eyes.
And when he saw his eyes were out,
  With all his might and main
He jumped into another bush
  And scratched them in again.

Gregory Griggs

Gregory Griggs, Gregory Griggs,
Had twenty-seven different wigs.
He wore them up, he wore them down,
To please the people of the town;
He wore them east, he wore them west,
But he never could tell which he loved the best.

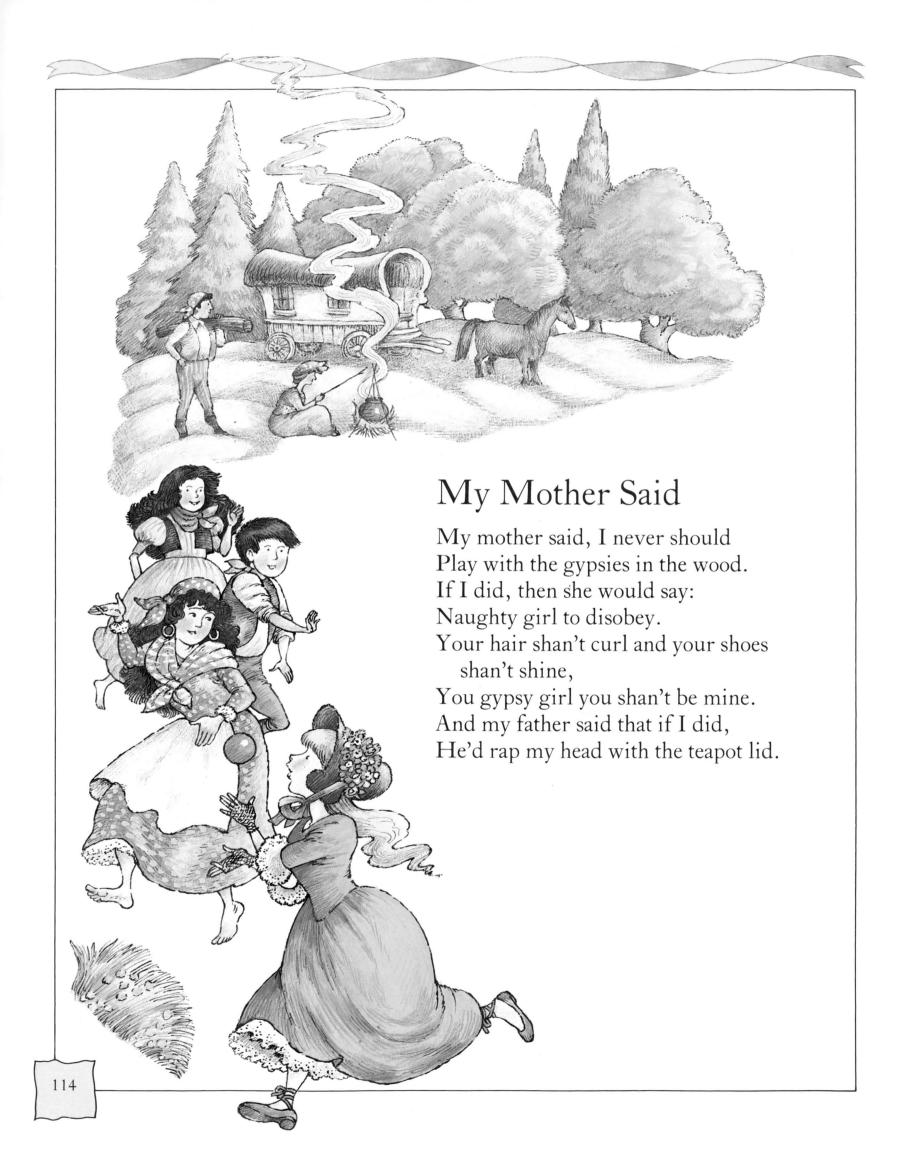

My Mother Said

My mother said, I never should
Play with the gypsies in the wood.
If I did, then she would say:
Naughty girl to disobey.
Your hair shan't curl and your shoes
   shan't shine,
You gypsy girl you shan't be mine.
And my father said that if I did,
He'd rap my head with the teapot lid.

Doctor Fell

I do not like thee, Doctor Fell,
The reason why I cannot tell;
But this I know, and know full well,
I do not like thee, Doctor Fell.

My Father Died

My father died a month ago
   And left me all his riches;
A feather bed, a wooden leg,
   And a pair of leather breeches;
A coffee pot without a spout,
   A cup without a handle,
A tobacco pipe without a lid,
   And half a farthing candle.

The Sky

Red sky at night,
Shepherd's delight;
Red sky in the morning,
Shepherd's warning.

Gunpowder Plot

Please to remember
The fifth of November,
Gunpowder treason and plot;
I see no reason
Why gunpowder treason
Should ever be forgot.

Pins

See a pin and pick it up,
All the day you'll have good luck.
See a pin and let it lay,
Bad luck you'll have all the day.

If Wishes
Were Horses

If wishes were horses,
    Beggars would ride.
If turnips were watches,
    I would wear one by my side.
And if "ifs" and "ands" were pots and pans,
There'd be no work for tinkers!

Three Ghostesses

Three little ghostesses,
Sitting on postesses,
Eating buttered toastesses,
Greasing their fistesses,
Up to their wristesses.
Oh, what beastesses
To make such feastesses!

Moses

Moses supposes his toeses are roses,
But Moses supposes erroneously;
For nobody's toeses are posies of roses
As Moses supposes his toeses to be.

Hannah Bantry

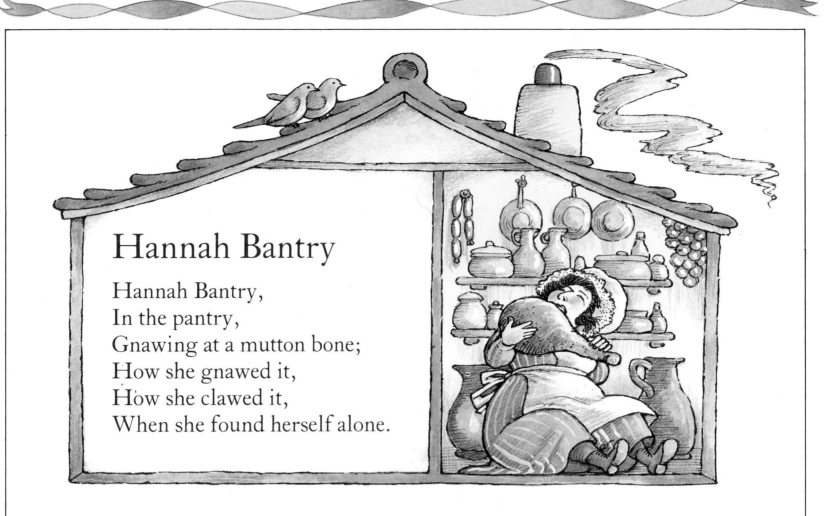

Hannah Bantry,
In the pantry,
Gnawing at a mutton bone;
How she gnawed it,
How she clawed it,
When she found herself alone.

The Owl

A wise old owl sat in an oak,
The more he heard the less he spoke;
The less he spoke the more he heard.
Why aren't we all like that wise old bird?

Cock Robin

Who killed Cock Robin?
I, said the Sparrow,
With my bow and arrow,
I killed Cock Robin.

Who saw him die?
I, said the Fly,
With my little eye,
I saw him die.

Who caught his blood?
I, said the Fish,
With my little dish,
I caught his blood.

Who'll make his shroud?
I, said the Beetle,
With my thread and needle,
I'll make the shroud.

Who'll dig his grave?
I, said the Owl,
With my pick and shovel,
I'll dig his grave.

Who'll be the parson?
I, said the Rook,
With my little book,
I'll be the parson.

Who'll be the clerk?
I, said the Lark,
If it's not in the dark,
I'll be the clerk.

Who'll carry the link?
I, said the Linnet,
I'll fetch it in a minute,
I'll carry the link.

Who'll be chief mourner?
I, said the Dove,
I mourn for my love,
I'll be chief mourner.

Who'll carry the coffin?
I, said the Kite,
If it's not through the night
I'll carry the coffin.

Who'll bear the pall?
We, said the Wren,
Both the cock and the hen,
We'll bear the pall.

Who'll sing a psalm?
I, said the Thrush,
As she sat on a bush,
I'll sing a psalm.

Who'll toll the bell?
I, said the Bull,
Because I can pull,
I'll toll the bell.

All the birds of the air
Fell a-sighing and a-sobbing,
When they heard the bell toll
For poor Cock Robin.

121

Index of First Lines

123